A LITTLE SPOT OF LOVE

Written & Illustrated
by Diane Alber

To my children, Ryan and Anna:
You grow my LOVE SPOT every day!

EVERYONE NEEDS TO BE LOVED!

WHAT GROWS A
LOVE
SPOT?

Hi! I'm a little SPOT of LOVE!

I'm the feeling you get when you care about someone, or when someone cares about you, **A LOT!**

I come from A LOT of feelings
and emotions...

And I can get pretty BIG!

But that's okay, because you never can have too much LOVE!
AND EVERYONE NEEDS TO BE LOVED!

When your LOVE SPOT is BIG,
you feel great about yourself, and you treat people
better! That's why I want to show you all the ways
you can GROW a LOVE SPOT!

Let's start with WORDS!

WORDS are VERY POWERFUL.
Saying how you feel or saying something nice can help someone feel LOVED.

I LOVE YOU!

COMPLIMENTS can grow a LOVE SPOT!

YOU ARE SMART!

YOU HAVE A GREAT SMILE!

Sometimes it's hard to say how you feel, and it's easier to write it out! Getting a surprise note or letter can help someone feel LOVED.

WORDS can also help you LOVE who you are, too!
CONFIDENCE can help grow a LOVE SPOT.

Today is a new day! I will have a great start.
I will listen to the voice inside my heart.
I will let good thoughts inside my mind
and tell myself: I am brave, I am loving, I am kind.

In addition to using WORDS,

ACTIONS are another way
to show you care.

When you take the time to DO something for someone
else, it makes them feel LOVED!

KINDNESS can grow a LOVE SPOT.

Spending QUALITY TIME with someone can make them HAPPY and show them that they are important. To show someone focused attention, make sure...

Your eyes are watching.
Your hands are still.
Your mouth is closed.

LISTENING can grow a LOVE SPOT.

There are times when it's fun to be silly and giggly with someone, too! You can play a game or just hang out!

FRIENDSHIP can grow a LOVE SPOT.

Take TIME to find things YOU enjoy, too.

Finding your
PEACEFUL SPOT
can help you grow
your OWN
LOVE SPOT.

Receiving something from the HEART can help someone feel APPRECIATED.

GIFTS can grow a LOVE SPOT.

There are many ways to show affection
when growing a LOVE SPOT!

HUGS can grow a LOVE SPOT.

HIGH FIVES can grow a LOVE SPOT!

FIST BUMPS can grow a LOVE SPOT!

WAVING can grow a LOVE SPOT!

Giving a THUMBS UP can grow a LOVE SPOT!

Now that you have seen all the ways you can GROW a LOVE SPOT, it's important to know that everyone likes to be LOVED DIFFERENTLY. For example, some people like HUGS, and some would rather have a HIGH FIVE.

So, I would LOVE to know...

WHAT IS YOUR FAVORITE WAY TO GROW YOUR LOVE SPOT?

WORDS
COMPLIMENTS
SAYING "I LOVE YOU"

ACTIONS
LISTENING
HELPING
BEING KIND

QUALITY TIME
PLAYING GAMES
READING
LISTENING

AFFECTION
HUGS
HIGH FIVES
FIST BUMPS
THUMBS UP

GIFTS
ART CREATIONS
CRAFTS

Write it here:

_____

_____

_____

WORDS
COMPLIMENTS
SAYING "I LOVE YOU"

ACTIONS
LISTENING
HELPING
BEING KIND

WHO GREW YOUR LOVE SPOT TODAY?

QUALITY TIME
PLAYING GAMES
READING
LISTENING

AFFECTION
HUGS
HIGH FIVES
FIST BUMPS
THUMBS UP

GIFTS
ART CREATIONS
CRAFTS

WORDS
COMPLIMENTS
SAYING "I LOVE YOU"

ACTIONS
LISTENING
HELPING
BEING KIND

QUALITY TIME
PLAYING GAMES
READING
LISTENING

DID YOU GROW A LOVE SPOT TODAY?

AFFECTION
HUGS
HIGH FIVES
FIST BUMPS
THUMBS UP

GIFTS
ART CREATIONS
CRAFTS

HOW DO YOU LIKE TO BE GREETED?

High Five

Fist Bump

Wave

Thumbs Up